This book belongs to:

_____

_____

This edition published by Parragon Books Ltd in 2016
and distributed by

Parragon Inc.
440 Park Avenue South, 13th Floor
New York, NY 10016
www.parragon.com

Written by Margaret Wise Brown
Edited by Xannaeve Chown & Lily Holland
Production by Juliet Fountain

Illustrated by Linda Bleck
Designed by Anna Madin

ISBN 978-1-4723-9221-3

Printed in China

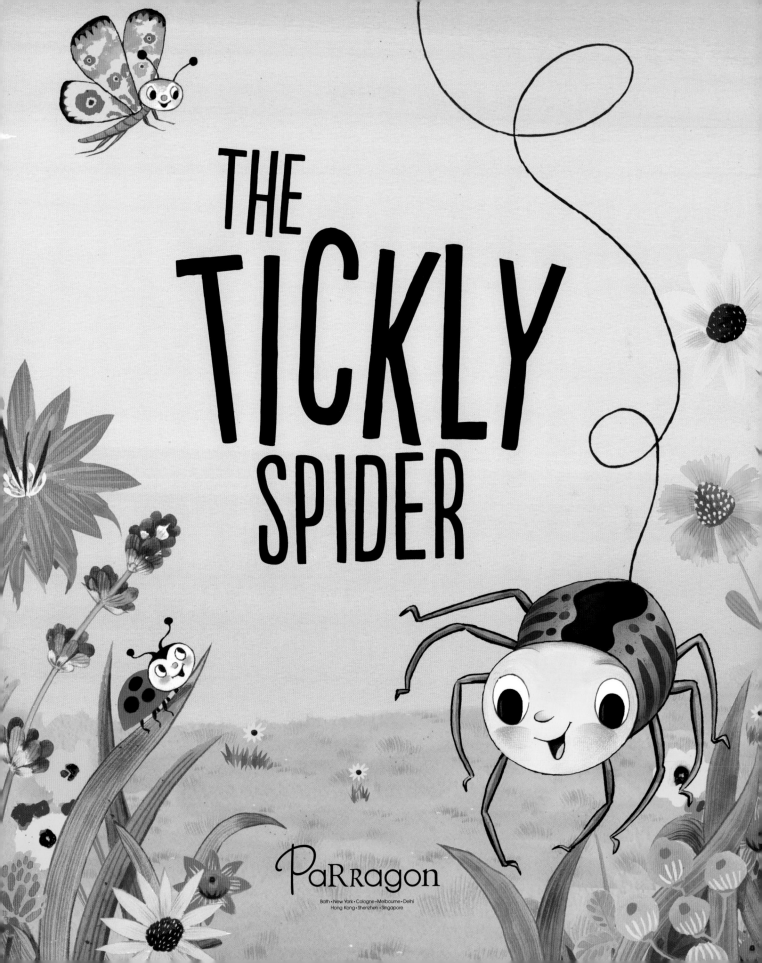

THE TICKLY SPIDER

PaRragon

Bath · New York · Cologne · Melbourne · Delhi
Hong Kong · Shenzhen · Singapore

A little spider lived deep in the grass at the edge of a field, about three buttercups away from where a little boy was lying on his tummy.

The little boy was peering in between the long, green grass blades.
Deep, deep, deep in the grassy wilds, the little boy looked.
And as he watched, he saw strange things ...

He saw a red ladybug climbing a stalk of grass very slowly.
He saw the shadow of a butterfly. And then ...

... in and out and around the grass stems came the little spider!

Over a root ...

... and over a twig.
Lugging and puffing along it came,
as little spiders come.

The spider was coming straight toward the little boy, winding in and out of the grasses. But the boy knew just what to do. He was a little boy who knew how to be very still.

The boy knew that if he kept stone still, the spider would only walk across him.

He was just like a **big hill** to the spider, a big hill that had to be climbed to get to the grass on the other side.

When the spider came to the last blade of grass in front of the little boy's nose, it stopped.

Then it began to climb.

It **climbed** and it climbed, until the grass bent toward the little boy's cheek ...

It jumped right into the hollow under the little
boy's eye. But the little boy stayed very still.

TICKLY, TICKLY,

the little spider started down
the little boy's cheek.

Tickly, tickly, past his nose.

Tickly, tickly, by the corners
of his mouth.

Even though it tickled like a million feathers,
the little boy lay as quiet as a stone.

Then the little boy didn't feel any more tickling.
He lifted his head slowly and saw the happy little
spider crawling off through the grasses.

Over a root ...

... and over a twig.

Lugging and puffing in and out and around the grass stems went the little spider.

And that was how the little boy stayed very still and saw a lot of things happening in between the long, green grass blades. Then, as the sun set, the little boy walked slowly home.

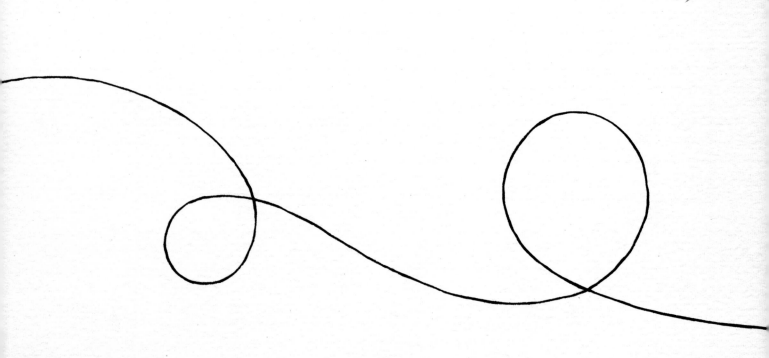